TO:

TRACE-

ALWAYS BE TRUE
TO YOURSELF!

Bali and Blu
Friends Of A Different Color

Deep in the jungle lived
an elephant named, Bali.
He was quite different
from the other elephants you see.

Bali did not like peanuts
or silly elephant games
and his best friend Blu,
was the size of a pea.

HEHEHE

HAHAHA

So often he was teased that it was even in his dreams he could hear the constant laughing of three.
"Just leave me alone," Bali silently wept, "I will make all you elephants see."

BWAHAHA

It was the next morning when
Bali awoke with a thought,
"I know just what to do - I'll
gather some brushes and a few
cans of paint and I will be green TOO!"

It was only when Bali was done
that he rushed to return to the herd.

With all eyes upon Bali, the older elephants laughed, "A green elephant - how absurd!"

Another elephant overheard
as she was walking by with her
trunk pointed high toward the sky.
"Friends with a grasshopper," she
sneered. "You must admit that it is
strange and it is weird!"

"Bali, you simply have
nothing in common
for it is obvious
to see - that this
friendship you share
just can not be!"

11

Bali sat with a thought,
a thought he never
thought before

"Perhaps they are right, to see a

GREEN

elephant is a funny sight!"

"Maybe wings would be better," Bali thought.
So, he put his plan into motion.

"Hmmmm, I'll use banana leaves
and stalks of bamboo -
just a few more things
and I will have wings TOO!"

All of a sudden Bali looked down
and saw that Blu was hopping by.
"What are you doing Bali?" Blu asked.
"Well, I am making wings." Bali smiled.

"Bali, you don't need wings
or to even be green.
Yes, we are different,
but we are friends anyway!"

It was right then that
Bali realized, it is not about
how tall or how small
if you fly or if you crawl.

He had a best friend
was all that Bali
knew, and yes it
was a grasshopper...a
grasshopper named Blu!

19

CPSIA information can be obtained
at www.ICGtesting.com
Printed in the USA
LVIC06n0348140817
544914LV00002B/4